Death of the Party

Written by Zack Carnahan

Edited by Justin Case

A very special thank you to my buddy Mojo.

You always go above and beyond. Your

help made this possible.

Table of Contents

<u>The Camping Trip!</u>

<u>Seance at Lucinda Grady's</u>

5

Party at Kirk's

Chapter 1

Crawling toward the door.

Covered in blood and disoriented.

The room was an eerie dark. Outside

the party was loud. Almost nothing

could be heard over the music. That

was why the screaming was

ineffective. In a futile tearful

attempt, she opened her mouth.

Nothing came but blood. Becky

Johnson was no more.

8: 00 p.m. the humble host

Kirk Smith was preparing for his

guests. He was having a party to

celebrate his new job. It was the

beginning of something exciting for

him and his stomach was full of

butterflies. The doorbell rang. It was his first guest. Becky Johnson entered with a vegetable tray.

Getting over the back fence was not enough. The terrifying juggernaut was rampaging toward him. He didn't see the branch. Frantically he scoured the ground looking for his glasses. A harsh snap from the darkness. Looking up he saw the outline of his demise and then nothing. Chuck Anderson was dead.

By 8:30 p.m. the party was going well. Becky Johnson was soon followed by Adam Brooks and his lovely wife Susan. Also, Hank Roberts and Jack Williams were there. Everybody had come except Kirk's good friend Chuck who would arrive by 8:45 p.m. It was such a great party and everybody was having fun. Kirk was almost forgetting the reason he left his old job. Tonight, was all about his future. Who he was to become.

Too much to drink. He just needed to lay down. The guest bedroom would be perfect. When he entered the room was spinning. He hit the floor. Slowly he clambered to his feet. The door was closed now. He did not remember closing it. The lights came on. An imposing figure overtook him. Blood seeped into the carpet. Jack Williams had left the party.

By 9:00 p.m. all of the guests were there. Mostly everybody was in the living room. Kirk saw Chuck go outside and Jack head upstairs but where was Becky? He asked around and nobody else had seen her. Then a scream. Susan Brooks saw her first. Becky was lying motionless in the laundry room. After the discovery Kirk rushed upstairs to tell Jack. There in the guest room, Kirk found him dead. By 9:15 p.m. two guests were murdered and one was missing. This party had become a nightmare. A horrified Adam Brooks was the first to call the cops. He was put on hold because all of the lines were busy. They would have to wait.

9:30 p.m. waiting for Chuck had become too much. Kirk had to go look for him. Alone, he mounted a search party. The rest stayed in the house, afraid what could happen.

Just a quick bathroom break. Nothing bad could happen there. The lights went out and it was pitch black. A cry was heard from the living room. Both Adam and Susan were dead. Lying together on the floor. Freaked out now, Hank ran outside. He slammed right into Kirk who was crying. Hank realized that Kirk was covered in blood. Kirk had found Chuck in the trees behind the house. Kirk and Hank ran down the street. Finally, they saw a neighbor. They called the police. The tragic night was over. The cops retrieved six dead bodies from the horror house. Becky Johnson, Chuck Anderson, Jack Williams, Adam and Susan Brooks. There were two survivors, Kirk Smith and Hank Roberts. They were both now in questioning.

Chapter 2

Room one, Kirk Smith. "Hello my name is officer Perry Jennings. I know you have had a rough night. I was just wondering would you like to explain your version of what happened tonight."

Officer Jennings asked Kirk. "Well we were having a party to celebrate my new job." Kirk explained. "Why did you get a new job? What happened at the old one?" Jennings probed for an answer. "Well I used to sell insurance. I had a couple come in trying to get a life insurance policy. The wife was too sick for forty-five to even consider her. She died of cancer and her husband couldn't pay for the funeral. He of course blamed me. I got a couple of threats and decided to leave to another job." Kirk finished. "What job is that?" Jennings asked. "I decided to write for the newspaper. After all my degree is in journalism."

Kirk replied with satisfaction. "Now please, back to your version of the story." Office Jennings ordered.

"Well the party was going great. Everybody was there by 9:00 p.m. Slowly everybody got comfortable. Chuck Anderson went outside, Jack Williams went to take a nap, and Becky Johnson was the only one I didn't see leave. When we noticed she was missing, we went looking for her." Kirk paused to drink the coffee in front of him. "Susan Brooks found Becky in the laundry room. After Susan found Becky Johnson, I ran upstairs to find Jack who I discovered was deceased in the guest room. I ran downstairs to tell everybody. At this time Adam Brooks called the police but the lines were busy so we waited. While waiting I decided to go find Chuck. Nobody wanted to come with me because they thought it was unsafe." Kirk again stopped to drink some coffee.

"I went out to the backyard and did not see Chuck. While looking around I saw my back gate was open. I went through it thinking Chuck would be there but, I didn't see him. I looked around and saw a red cup. That is when I found Chuck dead. At this point, I ran back to the house and ran into Hank Roberts. He told me that Adam Brooks and his wife Susan were dead. Instead of sticking around we took off. We got about five houses down before we saw a neighbor. We used his phone and called you." Kirk finished and took a drink. "Okay if there is anything else that comes to you let us know. Now if you would wait here while we question your friend." Officer Jennings spoke politely as he collected his folder and then exited the room.

Chapter 3

Room two, Hank Roberts. "Hello Mr. Roberts. My name is Officer Perry Jennings. And I'm going to ask you some questions." Officer Jennings spoke as he slid a cup of coffee in the direction of Hank Roberts. "How do you recall what took place tonight?" Jennings directed the question to an obviously distraught Hank. "Well Kirk was having a party." Hank paused to blow his nose. "What was the party for?" Asked Officer Jennings before Hank could continue. "Well Kirk said it was because he got a new job." Hank answered. "Why did he get a new job?" Jennings spoke as he looked down at a sheet of paper. "Well he said because he needed a new start. But when I asked Chuck, who worked with him at the insurance company, he said it was something else." Hank said while he was looking around. "And what was that reason?" Jennings pondered as he offered Hank a smoke. "Well Chuck said that Kirk wasn't doing well. He was in a drought and he wasn't getting any business. It really stressed him out. He became moody and easily agitated. The company had to let him go." Hank shook as he put down his cigarette and grabbed the cup of coffee from the table. "So you went to a party with a man who was moody and easily agitated?" An intrigued Officer Jennings asked. "Well I guess we are friends so I thought he needed it. I was only trying to help, not get wrapped up in the middle of a murder investigation." Hank said as he began to cry. "Then can you please continue?" Jennings spoke softly almost knowing that this might lead to some new details.

"Well I got there about 8:15 p.m. or so. Becky Johnson, Adam and Susan Brooks were already at the party. Soon after I arrived Jack showed up. I don't think Chuck came until maybe 8:45 p.m. I don't know exact times. I was already getting pretty smashed. At around 9:00 p.m. I think people started doing other stuff. Chuck went outside. I'm pretty sure Jack went upstairs to lay down because he wasn't feeling well. Fourteen shots will do that to you. Oh and Kirk and Becky went somewhere too. I heard from Chuck they had something going on. Well anyway something like 9:10 p.m. to 9:15 p.m. Kirk came back alone. He had a different shirt on. I can't be sure though, I was pretty gone by that time. An hour of drinking will put you in an odd place. Anyway, I remember us all looking for Becky after a while of not seeing her. I think Susan found her in the laundry room. I thought it was odd that Kirk didn't know where she was. After that he ran upstairs while me and the Brooks' waited downstairs. Kirk came down and said Jack was dead which is weird because I thought I heard the door close and then open a couple of minutes later. I don't know though it could have been the music. After that Adam called the cops." Hank paused to put out his cigarette and lit another.

"The line was busy so Kirk went outside to look for Chuck. I thought I saw Chuck by the back fence or something but then I had to puke so it could have been anything. I went into the bathroom to clean up a bit. Now I thought I heard the backdoor close but I was looking for something in the medicine cabinet and could have just moved a pill bottle. Then I heard a scream. I ran out and the Brooks' were dead. I didn't see Kirk so I thought that I couldn't have heard the door shut. I ran outside and ran into Kirk who had blood on him. He said he found Chuck in the trees out back so we ran for it. We made it to a neighbor and called the cops. Next thing is I'm talking to you. That's it." Hank finished the story and the coffee with a big gulp. "That is very interesting. I will be right back." Officer Jennings said with curiosity in his voice as he exited the room.

"Where is Kirk?" A puzzled Officer Jennings asked aloud. "He had to go to the bathroom. He said the coffee shot right through him."

Another officer said still reading his newspaper. "Jim, I told you to watch him!" Jennings yelled as he went back to interrogation room two.

The officer stationed outside the door was not there. Jennings flung open the door with his gun drawn. Hank Roberts had his head laying on the table. Jennings checked his pulse and found that Hank was dead. Hank Roberts was now not a suspect. He was victim number seven and Kirk Smith was nowhere to be found.

Hide and Go Seek

Chapter 1

"Wow! You are far too beautiful to be working in a place like this." A man told the cashier. "Thanks, you are far too good looking to be shopping here." The woman behind the counter answered back. "My name is Tina. What's yours?" Tina asked the handsome and charming stranger. "Kyle, my name is Kyle. It is very nice to meet you Tina." Kyle smiled at Tina and she smiled back. "Hey Tina would you like go out some time?" Kyle worked his charm a little more. "Definitely! Um, I get off in twenty minutes. You could come with me to a party I'm going to. It's going to be super fun!" Tina gave Kyle a big smile and did her best to try to persuade him.

"Alright that sounds great. Hey do you mind turning that up?" Kyle transitioned as he noticed a breaking story on the TV behind Tina. "Tonight, police are looking for a man named Kirk Smith. He is believed to have killed seven people yesterday evening at a house party and he is still at large. Police are asking for any details anyone may have of this man. All police have given is a name but they have not released a photo yet. When they do or if any further details are known we will bring you the breaking news." An anchorwoman reported in a serious tone. "Oh, that is terrible!" Tina shouted. "Don't worry I'm sure it's miles away. And hey, I'm here to protect you." Kyle tried to reassure the young woman. "Thanks. I feel much better. Are you ready to get out of here stud?" Tina said very happy she had somebody with her.

Chapter 2

"Hey guys, this is Kyle. I met him at work." Tina told her friends very happy to be showing that she brought somebody. "Cool man, welcome." One of Tina's friends reacted as he reached out to hand Kyle a beer. "So Kyle, I don't know

if Tina told you what we are doing."
The same man spoke again as he sat
back in his chair. "I thought it was a
party." Kyle answered. "Yeah, kind
of. Okay so once a month we all get
together. Oh shoot I totally forgot
you don't know anybody. I'm James.
That is Lisa." James paused. "Hey."
Lisa got up and shook Kyle's hand.
"That is Brad and Cameron on the
couch." James continued. "Hey man
what's up?" Brad asked as he shook
Kyle's hand while Cameron just
nodded in Kyle's direction. "And
finally, there is Steve who is
currently hammering home a taco."
James finished introducing the group
as Steve and Kyle shook hands.

"Okay, where was I?" James asked trying to retrace his steps. "The game." Tina chimed in with a big grin. "Ah yes, the game. Okay Kyle it is like hide and go seek but way more fun." James took a sip of beer before really trying to sell the game. "It's a game where one person is decided as the killer and they get a mask and a fake knife. They look around and chase everybody all through the house until they are all "dead". The last person to die will be the killer in the next round." James finished with a big smile and looked right at Kyle. "It's so much fun!" James added very excited to add somebody new to the game. "Alright house rules dictate that because you are the new guy, you get to be the killer. Let's put down some rules." James said looking around the room for volunteers to jump in. "First we have to turn off the lights and disconnect the phone. We want it to be as scary and real as possible." Steve jumped in while he grabbed more food. "Oh, everybody also has to hide alone so that way there are no distractions." Steve added between bites of taco. "And the killer must start off in the garage where they give everybody ten minutes to get hidden and make sure everybody is ready." Brad said still seated next to Cameron on the couch. "Then after the wait, the killer can do what they do. Stalk your prey and kill your victims." Tina spoke very seductively to Kyle. "Oh and one thing is if you break the record of kills, which is everybody dead within sixty-seven minutes, you will get one hundred dollars." James finished the rules as he slapped the money on the table. "Are you in?" James asked without really giving him the option to say no. "Sure, sounds fun." Kyle sounded a little hesitant.

"Should we do this? You know with the news story and all? It feels a little too real with an actual killer on the loose." Lisa said with fear in her voice. "Don't worry about that. It's just a game and besides it's not as if Kyle is a real killer." James tried to console the terrified girl. "Definitely not. I don't even watch scary movies." Kyle tried his best to calm everybody down after feeling eyeballs on him. "Okay Kyle go to the garage. Once the door closes, the clock starts." James said with a very big smile as he handed Kyle the mask and the knife.

Chapter 3

"Hey man let's hide together so we can finish this." Brad told his buddy Cameron as he passed him a joint. "Sure man. Let's go in here." Cameron spoke as he took a hit and pointed to a room nearby. "Hey guys get out of here. I'm hiding here." Tina whispered at the pair as they entered. "Okay. Let us just finish this. It shouldn't take too long." Brad whispered back as he hid behind the curtain by the window. "Oh man I think that guy is coming I hear footsteps." Cameron added in as he ducked behind the back of the door within handoff distance to Brad.

"Hey where did everybody hide?" Steve asked the empty dark house. "I really don't want to hide alone? Is anybody upstairs?" Steve asked as he began to climb. "Hey who is that?" He asked to the shape at the top of the stairs. "Oh. Hey Kyle man, I guess you got..." Steve couldn't finish the thought before he was pushed backwards down the stairs. He landed in a broken mass. He knew he had broken ribs if not worse. Steve looked up and saw the shape start to descend down the steps towards him. Then James' voice could be heard coming from upstairs. The figure stopped and turned around moving swiftly towards the sound. Steve was able to crawl towards another room where a television had been left on.

"Hey Lisa, are we ever going to get back together?" James asked Lisa in the upstairs bedroom. "Not while we are in the middle of a game. He is going to find us." Lisa responded obviously annoyed. "It's just that I miss you." James added. "If you continue to talk, I'm leaving." Lisa sternly spoke while trying to crouch down. "Lisa…" James began to speak but Lisa cut him off. "That's it. I hear him. Now I've got to hurry." Lisa shot James a dirty look and tried to exit the room but bumped into the masked killer.

"What? Hey psycho it's supposed to be a fake knife!" A tearful Lisa screamed. The cries were silenced by the big figure. He dragged the body out of the room and into the hall. "Hey wow! That's dedication." James told Kyle as he slapped him on the back. "Put Lisa's body in the garage to wait for the others." James smiled at Kyle as he moved down the hall with Lisa's body. "Oh yeah, The Killer got Lisa! Oh no!" James yelled as he entered another room further down the hall.

After depositing Lisa's corpse in the garage, the masked man came across all of the noise being made by Brad, Tina, and Cameron. The masked figure entered the room with fury. He opened the door slightly and slammed it back onto Cameron who let out a cough. "Hey man, what are you doing?" Brad asked as he stepped away from the curtain. Without answering, the killer's knife was thrust into the bottom of Brad's mouth. While this happened, Tina started to cry. She did her best to go for the door but was grabbed from behind. Cameron pushed the masked man hard enough to free Tina and she escaped.

Tina ran upstairs crying and ran into the room that James was now hiding in. "Hey, it's only a game." James did his best to try to calm Tina down as she entered visibly shaken. "Why are you crying?" James continued as he hugged her. "It's no game! I watched him kill Brad!" Tina cried out. "I know in the game. He got Lisa too. It's just lucky we got away." James was joking around and took the whole situation lightly.

Then from downstairs, a shriek of terror. "Hey wow. Good job Tina, this guy is a natural. Already three kills!" James was very excited. "I think he is a keeper. Okay, who is left? Me, you, and Steve I think?" He continued without really listening to Tina. "Are you nuts?! Kyle is killing them! Lisa is dead. Brad is dead. Right now, he is killing Cameron. We have to get out of here!" Tina's whisper was becoming a yell.

The sound of footsteps came towards them. The masked man crashed through the door. "Dude!

Don't destroy my house! You are paying for that…" James was interrupted as the man grabbed him. Tina took this opportunity to run. She heard James cry out in pain but could do nothing for him. She had to find Steve.

"Wait, come back." A voice called to Tina as she ran by a door downstairs. "Oh Steve, you are alive!" Tina whispered as she entered the room. "Kyle is killing people." Tina cried. "I know but his name isn't Kyle. It's Kirk something. He is that guy on the news." Steve spoke while grimacing in pain. "He attacked me first. He threw me down the stairs and I was able to crawl in here." Steve continued. "That's terrible. But how do you know he is this Kirk guy?" Tina asked while checking the hallway. "I saw the TV on and it was a breaking news report. It showed a photo and it was Kyle." Steve told Tina while grabbing his leg. "Why didn't you call the cops?" Tina was very upset as she questioned. "We disconnected the phone, remember? And I can't really get around to look for it." Steve paused to take in a strained breath. "I have just been waiting for somebody else to come in and I heard you crying. Is anybody else alive?" Steve asked through clinched teeth. "No. I don't think so. What do we do?"

Tina was shaking now and had panic in her voice. "Well you need to go get the cops. I guess I'll just stay here because I would only slow you down. Go get them so they can stop this guy." Steve said frustrated because he knew it was the only solution. "Wait. That makes no sense. If you stay you will die. There must be another way." Tina was full on crying now. "There is not. Lets just hope you can get to the cops before he can get away. Now go! I hear him moving around. It won't be long before he comes down stairs. You have to do this." Steve almost yelled at her. "Alright. I'll get to a neighbor's house and I'll call the cops. But then I'm coming right back for you." Tina said as she left the room.

Chapter 4

Steve waited in the room for a long time. He hoped that Tina had made it but as the gap in time widened, he began to get worried. Perhaps she was too scared to come back. Wouldn't he be? Then from somewhere in the house Steve heard a scream. Then the sound of broken glass. Then silence. It had to be Tina. Why would she come back? She had made it Steve thought to himself and felt guilt. The only question was, did she get to the cops? Now Steve truly was alone and he was immobile for the most part. All he could do was hope that the cops would be coming. His thoughts were interrupted. He heard footsteps come towards him. What would he do? He looked around the room and saw nothing on first glance. Then quietly he looked through the drawers of the desk he was hiding behind. Success. He found a letter opener. It was as good of a chance as he would get. The footsteps paused as a door was ripped open. Then they continued down the hall. Steve knew Kirk was searching each room. The sound of sirens was picking up in the distance. Tina did it and Steve may have a chance. The search grew louder and more rapid. The sirens grew louder and closer. Kirk was louder and closer. Then the sound stopped and the door Steve was hidden behind was ripped from its hinges. Kirk's silhouette filled the door.

"Breaking news tonight. Bodies found at a house in the hills. A grizzly scene of blood and carnage. Five bodies were discovered tonight at the house of James Wilson. The victims including Mr. Wilson, Steve Holmes, and Tina Henderson were believed to have been murder by a mask assailant that may or may not have been Kirk Smith, the man who is believed to have perpetrated similar crimes earlier this week. Police have not released any further information about the murders and no other victims' names have been released at this time as their corpses were badly mutilated and have not been identified. If this is Kirk Smith then we may be looking at more heartache and pain until this madman is captured. We will have more news at 11:00 p.m." A news anchor told his listeners as Kirk turned off the radio in his car and opened a beer. He smiled as he sped down the road into the darkness. Ready again for the thrill of the hunt.

The Thompson Wedding

Chapter 1

Her face had never looked so happy and when she looked at Donovan, she knew he felt the same. Sometimes you just know when you are going to spend the rest of your life with someone and Miranda knew that she had found that.

It was a beautiful church and all of their family was there. The crowd was slowly clearing out as the wedding was to shift to the reception which was a boat cruise in the harbor. It was going to be so amazing. Nothing but the big moon in the sky and the love between them.

There was only one real problem and that was that Donovan was not good with boats. He was prone to seasickness. In all of the chaos of a morning of a wedding day, Donovan's anti-nausea pills had been left at home. "It's no big deal. I'll just go grab them on our way." Donovan told Miranda. "We can't be late." Miranda pleaded with him. "Do you need them?" Miranda asked. "Do you want me puking over the side of the boat in the wedding album?" Donovan replied while eating a handful of candy. "Hey it's fine. I'll go." Miranda's maid of honor Claire offered the solution. "Oh wow. Really?" Miranda responded. "Yeah, it's really no problem." Claire replied. "Hey thanks! I really appreciate that. You are my hero!" Donovan jumped in and gave Claire a big hug. "Here is the key and the pills should be on the counter in the kitchen." Donovan spoke as he handed over his keys.

"Just make sure you are at the boat by 8:00 p.m. or the it will leave without you." Miranda added and hugged Claire.

Chapter 2

It was getting late and the pills were not on the counter. Claire was speeding through the night trying to make it to the boat before she couldn't get on. There was a bang and the car shifted. Claire had picked up a flat tire. "Perfect." Claire said to no one in particular. She pulled over the car and sat for a moment. Then she popped the trunk and started to look for what she needed to fix the situation. With tools in hand, Claire began to use the jack to lift up the car. While she loosened the lug nuts on the rim a car pulled up.

"Hey excuse me ma'am. Could you use some help?" The handsome driver of the other car asked. "Sure could stranger." Claire answered with a small smile. "Your damsel's name is Claire. Who might her hero be?" Claire flashed a big smile as she held out her hand. "Your hero this evening is Kevin." Kevin responded with a smile as he kissed Claire's hand.

"Where are you headed dressed so fancy?" Kevin asked as he took off the flat tire. "Oh my friend's wedding reception." Claire answered almost sounding annoyed. "It is so boring having to do all of this wedding stuff. I have had no one to talk to." Claire continued. "Yeah it can suck but you are there to make the bride happy." Kevin spoke as he tightened the lug nuts on the spare tire. "I know but still, do I have to be so bored?" Claire pouted at Kevin. "Hey I know, why don't you come with me?" Claire got excited as she thought of the idea. "Well that sounds fun, but I wouldn't want to impose." Kevin said as he closed the trunk of Claire's car. "No not at all. You would be doing me a huge favor. Besides my friend won't mind." Claire tried to look cute to try to persuade him. "Open bar?" Kevin asked with a grin. "Uh huh." Claire teased back. "Well I guess I can swing by. You know, for a minute." Kevin smiled. "So I'll follow you?" Kevin continued.

Chapter 3

"Here are your pills and here is Kevin." Claire said with enthusiasm in her voice. "Thank you Claire. Hi Kevin."

Donovan responded as he took the pills in one hand and took Kevin's hand in the other. "Where is your darling wife?" Claire asked. "She is with her mother. I stayed over here just in case." Donovan spoke as he put a pill in his mouth. "I hate boats but I love my wife." Donovan joked to Kevin as he took a drink to get the pill down. "So how did you guys meet?" Donovan asked the pair. "He rode in on his white horse and helped me with my flat tire." Claire jumped in almost bragging. "It was no trouble but she did offer an open bar." Kevin laughed as he put his hand on Claire's shoulder. "Well Claire, sounds like I need to get this man a beer. You can go find my wife." Donovan told Claire as he began to lead Kevin towards the bar. "No. No. You have to go deal with your mother in law, I'll take Kevin." Claire laughed as she intercepted Kevin. "But you have to tell Miranda that you are here." Donovan pointed out as he grabbed Kevin. "It's my wedding day today you know." Donovan added. "Well you do raise a fair point. You guys have fun." Claire folded as she patted Donovan's shoulder. "Thank you. I love you!" Donovan responded as he and Kevin disappeared into the dining room of the boat.

Chapter 4

"Hey let's get these beers to go! I got a great spot." Donovan told Kevin. "Sounds great." Kevin responded as he took a knife from the bar while Donovan was getting drinks. "Yeah if we go to the back of the boat nobody should bug us." Donovan motioned for Kevin to follow. The pair found some chairs at the back of the boat. "So Kevin, what do you do?" Donovan asked as he drank. "I'm a banker." Kevin responded. "Dang maybe that's it. I feel like I've seen you." Donovan said as he peered at his new friend. "Perhaps you've seen me on TV?" Kevin asked. "I've been on it quite a bit over the last few months." Kevin continued. "Oh yeah? Moonlighting as an actor?" Donovan joked. "Something like that." Kevin smiled. "Oh snap! Oh no dude, I know what it is. You look like that killer dude." Donovan looked concerned as he started to piece it together. "Exactly." Kevin stood up. "My name is Kirk Smith." Kirk said with a devilish smile. Donovan tried to get up and while he did Kirk grabbed

Donovan. Kirk plunged the knife into Donovan's chest. Donovan spit up blood onto Kirk's face.

"Yo Don! What up?" A voice from behind them spoke. "Reg!" Donovan barely got it out. "Oh shit!" Reggie yelled. He tried to run to get help, but he slipped. Reggie hit his head on the railing of the boat. Kirk walked up to Reggie's body and picked up the man's head. He smashed it on the deck of the ship and threw Reggie into the water. Kirk then walked over and threw Donovan overboard and into the darkness. Kirk wiped off his face, finished his drink, and went back to the party.

"Hey girl!" Claire called out to Miranda as she approached. "Oh good, you made it!" Miranda answered back. "I was worried that you hadn't. The boat started moving and I hadn't heard from you." Miranda continued. "Yeah I made it and I got Donovan his pills." Claire smiled back. "Where is my husband anyway?" Miranda questioned as she looked around the boat. "Oh, he is with Kevin." Claire responded. "Kevin?" Miranda asked with a smirk. "Kevin is a guy that helped me out. See while I was saving the day, I got a flat tire speeding over here and Kevin helped me out." Claire explained.

"My ears were burning." Kirk spoke as he entered from behind the women. "Oh hey! Miranda, this is Kevin. Kevin, this is Miranda." Claire exclaimed in happy amusement. "Hey Kevin nice to meet you. Thanks for taking care of my girl." Miranda shook his hand and smiled. "And your boy unfortunately. Donovan isn't feeling well I'm afraid." Kirk responded. "Damn. Did he not take the pills in time?" Miranda asked. "I guess not. I can take you to him if you would like." Kirk did his best to try to console Miranda. "Sure. Claire, would you stay here and tell my mom where I'm at?" Miranda pleaded as she began to follow Kirk. "Sure, but don't forget about me." Claire agreed with concern in her voice.

Kirk guided Miranda towards the back of the boat with his knife at the ready. "Hey, where is Donovan?" Miranda questioned. "He was just over here. Maybe he fell in?" Kirk suggested. Miranda went to the railing and looked into the water. Kirk seized the opportunity and grabbed Miranda from behind. Miranda started to scream but Kirk covered her mouth with one hand and slit her throat with the other. Miranda's blood spilled out all over her white dress. Kirk dumped her body over the railing into the same watery grave as her husband.

"Hey Kevin, I couldn't take it. Miranda's mom just wouldn't stop talking to everybody. I just decided to come find you guys." Claire spoke to Kirk's back. Kirk was still by the railing he had just dropped Miranda over and his arm was covered in blood. Almost as soon as he realized there was blood, Claire noticed that a pool had formed at Kirk's feet. "Hey Kevin, where are Donovan and Miranda?" Claire timidly asked. "They are at the bar. I just came out here to clear my head." Kirk answered with his back still to Claire. "Why don't you come over here. I want to show you something." He spoke coldly as he wiped the bloody knife on his jacket. "No, I think I'll just go to the bar." Claire trembled as she backed up and away from Kirk. "Come here!" Kirk demanded. "No!" Claire yelled and started to run. Kirk spun around and began to pursue her.

Claire made it into the dining room and she was crying. "Whoa are you okay?" The bartender asked. "No! There is a man. My date Kevin, who just killed the bride and groom!" Claire was crying and the words barely came out. Just then Kirk entered the room consumed with rage and was in a full sprint. Claire ducked behind the bar and hid behind the bartender. The bartender grabbed an ice pick to defend Claire. Kirk got behind the bar with his knife drawn. The two men squared off both positioning themselves for the fight. Kirk kicked the bartender into Claire and they fell to the ground. Kirk then kicked the ice pick out of the bartender's hand as Claire struggled to try to get up. She was pinned by the bartender. Kirk stabbed the bartender multiple times with his knife. Blood squirted everywhere and Claire kicked and punched at Kirk as she tried to free herself. Kirk picked her up by her hair and held the knife to her throat. Claire punched Kirk's face and kicked him in the knee. He let go and she clambered over the bar and fell onto the floor.

There was no one in the dining room to help. Claire tried to get up to get to the front of the ship. She couldn't get her feet under her so she crawled. Kirk had made his way from behind the bar and grabbed Claire by the ankle as she grabbed the door. Kirk pulled her towards him and planted the knife in her stomach. Her eyes widened and she let out a gasp. Kirk stabbed her a few more times until blood poured from the wound and from her mouth. Kirk realized that he was now covered in blood and had to get through the party to get off of the boat.

Just as he was pondering his options a waiter walked in. Kirk picked up a candlestick holder from the table nearby. "Oh god! What happened in here?" The waiter asked. "Don't worry about it." Kirk told the man as he walked over to check on him. Kirk hit the waiter in the head and put on the man's clothes. Kirk slipped out of the dining room and into the crowd just as the boat was docking. Kirk walked past Miranda's mother and winked with a smile on his face. He left the boat and disappeared into the night not even knowing himself where his path of destruction would lead him next.

The Camping Trip!

Chapter 1

It was finally Spring and the weather was starting to warm up. In fact, the weather was perfect for a camping trip. Or so Ray thought. He had convinced his girlfriend Gloria to go and she talked Finn, Darcy, Margot, and even her brother Alfred to go. Just a couple of days and a couple of great friends spending time together sleeping under the stars.

"Margot you promised you would go." Gloria said to Margot as she packed. "And I will. I just have to go on a date." Margot explained. Gloria didn't even have the words to express her displeasure so she settled for rolling her eyes instead. "What? He was super cute." Margot did her best to defuse the situation. "Look, I will go on the date and I will just meet you guys up there tomorrow." Margot continued and then put on some lipstick. "But you promised." Gloria complained and pouted her lip. "And I will be there. It will just be one day later." Margot tried to comfort her best friend with a hand on her shoulder. "Besides, I'm sure Ray will do all he can to get lucky tonight so I'm sure your dance card is full." Margot joked. "Okay, wish me luck. See you tomorrow." Margot hugged Gloria and left the apartment.

Three honks was the sign. Gloria grabbed her stuff and headed downstairs. She opened the door and looked in. Crammed in the back of the van was Finn by himself with Alfred and Darcy in the row in front of him. "You get shotgun. Hey where is Margot?" Ray asked from the driver's seat. "She has a date." Gloria spoke softly and was obviously upset. "Looks like Ray isn't the only one getting laid tonight!" Finn yelled from the back of the van. "Finn you're such an idiot." Darcy said in a disappointed tone. "Can we just go?" Gloria asked the group annoyed. "Yeah, just hop on board. We are going to have so much fun!" Ray told Gloria as he leaned out of the window for a kiss. "Just drive." A very grumpy Gloria spoke as she climbed into the back and motioned to Alfred to move. "Guess I got shotgun." Alfred exclaimed as he climbed through the van and into the front seat. "Alright family, Let's go." Ray told the group in a deflated tone.

Chapter 2

It was going to be a long drive up to the campsite and Ray knew it would feel a lot longer with Gloria upset. It was an hour in before they made their first stop. They were just about halfway there. "If I don't get out of this car, I am going to pee in it." Finn calmly spoke from the back. "It's only been an hour and we only have two left. Why don't we wait?" Ray told him. "I want to stop too." Gloria talked for the first time since they had left. Ray pulled over off of the highway and stopped at a gas station. "Thanks baby!" Finn sarcastically yelled to Ray. "That's right, I beat you to it." Finn joked to Gloria as he squeezed past her and exited the van. Gloria cracked a little smile. "See, feeling better already." Ray said as he held out his hand to help Gloria out of the van. The two of them walked into the gas station arm and arm leaving Darcy and Alfred alone.

"So you are Gloria's brother?" Darcy asked. "Yeah and you are one of her friends?" Alfred responded. "Yeah." Darcy answered back. "Well this is just awkward." Finn said as he returned to the van. "So Darcy, what is your deal?" Finn asked as he tried to squeeze onto the bench seat next to her. "Same as always Finn. Not into you." Darcy answered as she scooted down. "Besides later when we get drunk, I've got options now." Darcy jabbed at Finn as she nodded towards Alfred. "Oh come on baby. We both know who's tent you're ending up in." Finn spoke as he put his arm around

Darcy. "Sounds like mine." Alfred jabbed at Finn which prompted Darcy to smile. "Boys, what is a lady to do? Who wants to buy me some chips?" Darcy questioned as she got out of the van on the other side. Alfred and Finn both knew the math. Somebody was going to be very lonely tonight and they were both determined not to be the odd man out. "I got you." Alfred jumped in first. As he got out of the van to walk around, Finn slid across the seat. "Darcy, it would be my pleasure." Finn spoke to Darcy as he took her hand. "Hey Alfred, I think somebody should stay with the van and I've got to go help Darcy so…" Finn mocked Alfred as he and Darcy left. "Damn." Alfred muttered to himself as he sat back down.

Margot was very excited for her date. It had been a while and Keith was such a nice guy. Plus he was taking her to a fancy restaurant so she was pretty sure he was serious. Hopefully it could lead somewhere but just in case Margot met him at the restaurant so that way she would have her own car if it went bad. Keith was already waiting outside of the place when she arrived. "Hey." Keith said to Margot as he kissed her cheek. "Hey." Margot replied coyly as to not give away her excitement over the kiss. The pair then walked into the restaurant.

"Oh man was that steak good." Keith said as he put down his utensils. "I am full." He continued as he smiled at Margot. "Me too." Margot replied as she put her napkin on her plate. "Well I had a great time but I should really get going. I have a long drive in the morning." Margot continued before drinking more wine. "Oh yeah, what have you got going on?" Keith asked very interested. "I'm meeting my friends. They went camping and I said I would go. My friend Gloria is pissed that I'm not going to be there tonight but you were well worth it." Margot explained. "Camping? Man, I haven't done that in years. That sounds like a blast!" Keith eagerly responded. "You are going to have a great time." Keith added. "No not really. I get to watch Gloria and her boyfriend make out and I have to deal with Finn trying to bang me and then trying to get with Darcy when he strikes out." Margot told the scenario as if she had lived it a thousand times. "You know since camping sounds so fun, would you be willing to go with me?" Margot tried to sell it with her eyes. "You could be like my buffer." Margot finished the pitch and drank more wine. "I mean sure, why not?" Keith responded and drank from his own glass. "But hey, why wait until tomorrow? We can just go right now." Keith suggested. "Are you packed up?" He asked as he motioned to the waiter for the check. "Yeah, it's all in my car actually." Margot confirmed. "Great, we'll take your car. Can we swing by my place so I can grab a toothbrush and sleeping bag?" Keith sounded excited. "Absolutely!" Margot answered with a big smile.

Chapter 3

It was starting to get dark by the time they arrived at the campsite. Ray picked a spot that he felt was fairly isolated so that way they wouldn't be bothered by anybody. After all, this trip was supposed to be relaxing and he thought who wants to be around other people when camping is about escape. Ray, Alfred, and Finn put up the tents while Gloria and Darcy unloaded the rest of the van. "So, what do you think of Alfred?" Gloria asked Darcy as they lowered the ice chest of beer out of the van. "I don't know, I'm probably just going to stay with Finn." Darcy admitted as she grabbed a beer. "You always do this." Gloria rolled her eyes at Darcy. "What can I say? The sex is fun and I don't have to worry about commitment. We can have fun and by Tuesday it is onto a guy worth my full attention." Darcy spoke coldly and openly. "Dang that is cold." Gloria told her friend as she shook her head in disapproval as she got a beer also. "I don't know, I think you should give Alfred a shot." Gloria continued and then took a drink. "We'll see." Darcy said as she finished her beer.

"So, who is in the lead?" Ray asked to both of them. "Oh I am for sure." Finn chuckled as he stretched the pole from the top to the bottom of the tent. "I mean you do have the edge." Ray retorted as he began to put the stakes into the ground. "Winning is winning. Besides I don't think little bro has the stuff." Finn added as he tried to negotiate on what to do next to bring up the middle of the tent. "Oh, I wouldn't bet against me. Did you see how she was looking at me?" Alfred chimed as he sat in a chair outside of his completed tent. "In fairness, she looks at all men like she is shopping at a meat counter." Ray joked. "That is true and I just happen to be a product that brings in return customers." Finn gloated back. "That is because low quality is always on sale." Alfred jabbed at Finn. Finn mocked laughter in response. "Alright guys let's calm down." Ray tried to cool them down. "And I'm done. Finn you have to shotgun a beer." Ray said in victory after tackling the hieroglyphic instructions of his tent. Finn picked up a beer and just looked distraught at the status of his tent.

"Ladies, your hotel is open." Ray proclaimed to the women. "Why thank you sir. I will take a nonsmoking room." Darcy joked back. "Well then Alfred is certainly going to win." Finn chimed in while catching his breath from the beer. "Damn that's rough." Gloria laughed as she walked over. "What have we got to eat? I'm starving." Darcy asked Ray who had started a fire. "Oh I've got something." Finn jumped in before Ray could talk. "Easy there buddy. She said she was hungry not looking for an appetizer." Alfred fired the shot and got Darcy to flash a big smile. "Hey we may need more firewood. Who wants to go get it?" Ray asked and shot Finn a look in an attempt to cut off the joke before it started. "I'll go. Alfred can you assist me?" Darcy cheerfully volunteered. "Absolutely." Alfred smiled at Finn and took Darcy's arm and they disappeared into the woods.

"Wow we are making great time." Margot exclaimed looking at her watch. "Yeah I just need to stop and get some things. Do you mind?" Keith asked as he pulled into a gas station. "Just grab me an energy drink. I need to wake up a little." Margot said as she yawned. "Sure thing." Keith smiled as he exited the vehicle.

Margot decided to try to call Gloria. "Hello?" Gloria answered the phone. "Hey girl! So my date went great and Keith and I are coming up tonight!" Margot spoke excitedly into the phone. "Awesome! What time can we expect you?" Gloria asked.

"I'm not sure. Just keep doing whatever you guys are doing. We will be there when we can." Margot explained. "I'm so excited! Yay!" Gloria yelled. "See you soon, love you." Gloria finished. "Love you too. Bye." Margot said as they hung up their phones.

"Three energy drinks, a candy bar, and a hatchet. You must be having a fun night." The clerk joked with Keith. "Well just going camping." Keith answered back. "Hey you be careful out there. A lot of bad things can happen in the woods at night." The clerk spoke with a nice level of concern. "Oh I'm not worried, I'm going to be the scariest thing in those woods tonight." Keith joked with the man. "Well take care. You have a nice night." The clerk gave Keith his change and smiled. "Will do." Keith added as he nodded and left the store.

"So me and Alfred found a weird building in a clearing." Darcy told the group as she dropped an armful of branches. "It was a construction site. The building is only about six stories high." Alfred clarified as he also dropped a bundle of sticks. "It would be a great view from up there." He added as he stoked the fire. "Okay. Let me grab my coat." Gloria said as she went into her tent. "Hey Finn somebody should stay here, you know, to watch the campfire so…" Alfred mocked Finn as he stood up and put his arm around Darcy. "Actually yeah, somebody has to wait for Margot." Ray added inadvertently being a wingman to Alfred. "You guys suck." Finn grumbled from his chair. "You guys ready?" Gloria asked as

she popped out from the tent. "Let's go!

This is so exciting!" Darcy squeaked with

excitement. "It's going to get colder. Can we

take the van?" Gloria asked. "Sure we can.

Let's get a move on it." Ray spoke and the

four of them got into the van and drove

away leaving Finn to hang out by himself.

<u>Chapter 4</u>

"Wow this is cool!" Gloria yelled.

"Yeah I guess they are building everywhere

these days." Ray added. "Wait until we see

the view!" Darcy beamed. The four of them

took the elevator to the top. "It is beautiful."

Alfred said as he looked out. "Yeah." Ray

spoke while looking at Gloria. It really is."

Gloria responded as she looked at Ray. "Oh

shoot, I left my purse in the van. Alfred

want to go grab it with me?" Darcy looked

at Alfred. "Yes, let's do that." Alfred

responded understanding the look. "We are

going to give you guys some privacy." He

added. "You kids have fun." Ray joked as he

held Gloria as they looked out over the

woods. "You guys have fun." Darcy joked

as she and Alfred walked towards the

elevator.

"Margot! Thank god you are here."

Finn yelled as Margot approached from the

darkness. His attitude was slightly shifted as

Keith showed up behind her. "Oh and you

brought guests." Finn's tone changed.

"Where is everybody?" Margot asked as she

and Keith stepped closer to the fire. "Those

dicks left me here to wait for you." Finn

slurred his speech and had obviously been

drinking. "Hey buddy my name is Keith."

Keith reached out his hand to Finn who

slapped it and smirked. "Hey man, I'm

Finn." Finn responded and then drank from

the beer can in front of him. "So you guys

going to sit down or what?" Finn asked as

he kicked a chair next to him with his foot.

"Uh no, sorry. I'm going to go find Gloria."

Margot told her very drunk friend. "Keith

you coming?" Margot asked knowing Keith

craved a reprieve. "Oh thank god." Keith

said as he got closer to Margot. "Which

direction sir?" Margot questioned. "That

way and when you find them tell them I'm

not a happy camper." Finn started to laugh.

"Get it?" He continued to laugh until he fell

out of his chair. "Hey you guys be careful."

Finn spoke as he stood up and dusted

himself off. "Okay Keith, I've got to stay.
He is way too drunk. Can you go find my
friends?" Margot asked as she helped Finn
back to his chair. "Sure, I can totally go
walking in the woods at night, alone, to find
people I don't know." Keith spoke with as
much sarcasm as he could muster. "Thanks."
Margot said and completely ignored his
tone.

It had been an hour and Margot was
getting antsy. "I think he got lost." Margot
explained to Finn who was downing coffee
as where doctor's orders. "Well maybe we
should go find them." Finn replied between
big gulps of coffee. The two of them
grabbed flashlights and embarked. They
wandered around for a bit. It was more of a

hike than they expected. Then they found the van.

Alfred was laying among some rocks to the right side of the van. "Looks like Al struck out." Finn joked as they approached. "Hey Al! How did it go?" Finn called out. Margot and Finn got closer and realized that the van door was open and it was completely covered in blood. It was smeared from roof to floor with blood. "What the fuck?" Finn whispered. "Alfred what happened?" Margot bent down and touched Alfred's shoulder. He didn't move and when she pulled her hand back it was covered in blood. Margot turned Alfred over and found a deep cavern in his chest. "Oh my god!" Margot screamed. "That is not right!" Finn spoke as he looked down. "What the hell happened? What could have done that?"

Margot cried. "I don't know man. This isn't

right." Finn whispered back. "We've got to

find the others." Finn added. "Wait, what is

that sound?" Margot asked while she was

shaking.

The sound grew louder and got

closer. It sounded like rapid footsteps and

branches breaking. Then a bloody Keith

erupted from the woods. "Whoa!" Finn

yelled as he jumped back. "Keith?" Margot

squeaked up at her date. "Oh thank god you

guys are here." Keith muttered. "I've been

running around forever. I got lost. I found

the van and panicked." Keith continued.

"Are you okay? Are you hurt?" Margot

asked as she jumped up to hug Keith. "This

is messed up. I'm out of here." Finn blurted

out as he looked like he was going to leave.

"I'm going to get the cops." Finn told the plan to the group as it developed in his head. "Margot give me your keys." He added.

"Shoot. I left them at the campsite." Keith said. "I can go with Finn." Keith looked at Margot. "I'll get him the keys and come right back." Keith told Margot as she looked up at him. "Okay, I'm going to go find Gloria." Margot said with fear in her voice. "I won't leave her out here." She cried out.

"Hey check the construction site. I think they went over there to see the view from the top." Finn added in. "I'll take care of him and I'll be right back." Keith kissed Margot as he and Finn left. Margot ran towards the construction site with the hope that she would find Gloria.

Keith and Finn ran as fast as they could through the woods. It only took them half of the time to get back to the campsite that it took to get up to the van. "Okay where did you leave the keys?" Finn asked when they reached the camp. "Give me a second." Keith responded between big breaths. "It's been a while." He added with his hands on his knees. "Dude we don't have time." Finn stressed the urgency. "Oh they are right here." Keith stopped breathing heavy and pulled the keys from his pocket. "Dude what the fuck?" Finn questioned as Keith stood up straight. "Hey man. No way!" Finn yelled as he backed away. Keith pulled the hatchet from his jacket. "Finn. Buddy. Let's not make this harder." Keith spoke coldly. Finn turned to run but tripped over a rock. Before Finn could get to his feet Keith was standing over him. Keith buried the hatchet into Finn's chest and pulled it out rapidly. Blood misted the air. Keith wiped his face and headed back up the trail.

Margot reached the construction site and started to run up the stairs. She was so scared she ran right by the elevator. When she reached the top of the structure, she saw Gloria and Ray sitting on the ledge and looking out over the woods. "Gloria!" Margot yelled as she got close. "Margot!" Gloria yelled back with a big smile. She soon realized that Margot was not smiling and was in distress.

"Hey. Hey sweetie. What's wrong?" Gloria asked as she hugged Margot. "Somebody killed Darcy and Alfred!"

Margot cried. "We found the van, it was covered in blood." She continued as she broke down even more. "What? Alfred is dead?" Gloria cried out. "Who killed them?" Ray asked as he tried to console the distraught Gloria. "Hey babe. I'm so sorry." He said to Gloria as he struggled to keep her on her feet. "I don't know. Keith and Finn went to go get help." Margot responded as she joined the hug. "Who is Keith?" Ray asked as he put his arms around Margot as well. "He is my date. He is coming back once Finn gets the keys." Margot answered as she and Gloria continued to cry. Then the sound of the elevator started up. "Who is using the elevator?" Ray asked with genuine concern. "That is probably Keith." Margot wailed. She broke off from the hug and ran to the elevator to meet Keith.

The doors opened and Margot ran in and embraced Keith. He pushed her back and swung the hatchet. It sliced through her neck and her head left her shoulders. "Get behind me." Ray told Gloria who was still out of it. Keith stepped over Margot's body and rapidly approached the pair. Ray charged Keith who swung the hatchet at Ray. Keith missed and Ray tackled him to the ground. The two of them wrestled on the ground for a bit until Keith grabbed onto Ray's head and bounced it off of the ground. The blow knocked Ray unconscious. Keith got to his feet and grabbed the hatchet.

Keith walked towards Gloria slowly. He spun the hatchet in his hand to try to torment Gloria. It had a great effect because Gloria broke down crying and slumped to the ground. "Who are and what do you want?" Gloria screamed. "I am Kirk Smith and I'm here to kill you." Kirk said as he loomed closer and closer to Gloria. His back was to a stirring Ray. Ray got his bearings and he found a length of pipe on the ground near him. He sprang to his feet and made his way towards Kirk.

"I am that bad man that the news just can't get enough of." Kirk mocked as he was unaware of the developing situation behind him. He was now standing over Gloria with the hatchet over his head. He was ready to swing down on her. "But why us?" Gloria cried out. Kirk just smiled down at her and lowered the hatchet. "Because it's fun for me." Kirk joked as he raised his arms again. Ray hit the hatchet out of Kirk's hand. Kirk spun around to try to attack Ray who swung again and hit Kirk in the head. "Is it still fun?" Ray yelled at the madman. Kirk stumbled and Ray swung again. Ray had knocked Kirk closer to the edge of the building. "Hey man we can talk about this." Kirk spoke softly. Ray charged at Kirk who was unbalanced and Kirk plummeted off of the edge of the building and into the darkness. He landed onto a pile of cinderblocks that exploded and sent a dust cloud into the air. Ray looked down and Kirk was a bloody mess covered in rubble.

"Gloria are you okay?" Ray asked as he brought Gloria to her feet. "No, but I'm not hurt." Gloria cried up at Ray. "Is he dead?" Gloria managed to get the words out between tears. "I think so." Ray spoke calmly as he tried to comfort her. The couple walked to the edge to make sure. There, six stories down, was the body of Kirk Smith. He was dead and their nightmare was over. The only survivors of this horrible tragedy.

They both sat there holding each other until the sun brought the construction crew. They explained what had happened and the men gave them coffee and stayed with them until the police arrived.

"Hello my name is Perry Jennings. Can you tell me what happened here?" Officer Jennings asked the pair. "That Kirk Smith guy went on a date with my friend Margot and killed all of our friends." Gloria cried. "How did he end up down here dead?" Jennings asked her. "He tried to kill me and Ray kicked his ass." Gloria spoke and hugged Ray tighter. "You were able to fight him off?" Jennings asked surprised. "Yeah he went after my girlfriend. Why who is he?" Ray asked. "He is a serial killer who has racked up quite the body count recently. Honestly, you are lucky to even be alive." Jennings spoke with a little bit of pride. "Is that all officer? I'd really like to go home." Gloria asked Jennings. "Yeah, let's get you guys checked out and get you home. You have been through a lot." Jennings answered with a hand on Gloria's shoulder. "Hey take care of these two. They have been through the ringer." Officer Jennings told the paramedic as he walked by. "Ray thanks again. We have been after this guy for a long time. You have helped out a lot of families get closure. Let me know if there is anything I can do." Jennings shook Ray's hand and gave him his card. Officer Jennings smiled at them as he walked away towards the body of Kirk Smith. Ray and Gloria had no idea how lucky they were. The only two survivors of a rampage of blood, violence, and death.

Seance at Lucinda Grady's

Chapter 1

Gloria was just sitting on the couch watching bad late night TV. It was her new routine. She had found it incredibly difficult to get over that night. It was terrible to her that Margot was dead. After all, they had been friends for a long time. But it wasn't Margot being gone that kept her up nights it was the death of her brother Alfred. She just couldn't shake the sight of his body in that black bag being hoisted into the back of the coroner's van. It was Alfred by name but in her mind, there was no way it could be Alfred. Not her brother. He just could not be dead. They had way too much time left. It was not so long ago that they were playing outside or going to the drive-in movie theater. To summers at Grandma Sophia's house and late night conversations helping out with broken hearts.

It was not just longing for the fun times they shared but also it was the guilt. In the last few years they had grown apart. They just were not as close. Gloria felt responsible because it was her creating the distance. Between going to college, moving out with Margot, and her incredible relationship with Ray, Gloria made less and less time for Alfred. It was because of this that Gloria had invited him on the trip. In her mind she was just as guilty for getting him killed. If she hadn't begged him to go, he wouldn't have been dead. She abandoned him and then killed him. Gloria could not get over this. She felt with every fiber of her being that if she could, she would trade places with him in a heartbeat.

Ray too was having a hard time dealing with overcoming the ordeal. But for him it was more about Gloria. She was a shell of her former self and there just was nothing he could do to help. He tried to call but she would only pick up about half of the time. Gloria wouldn't even leave the house really unless it was to go to work so Ray had to go over there just to see her.

There was a knock on Gloria's door and she got up to get it. On the other side of the door was Ray and he was holding flowers. "Hey you." Ray smiled as he reached out to hand Gloria the flowers. "Hey." Gloria spoke almost uninterested as she turned to go back to the couch. "Are you doing any better today?" Ray asked as he entered the apartment and closed the door behind him. "No." Gloria huffed as she sat down. "I'm going to put these in some water for you." Ray tried his best to get a smile from her. "Fine." Gloria responded without enthusiasm. "Hey Gloria if there was anything I could do, you know I would do it." Ray said as he sat next to Gloria on the couch. "I love you and I know you are hurting but you are going to be okay." He continued as he leaned over and kissed her on the top of her head. "I love you too." Gloria spoke in a sweet way to acknowledge that she was listening.

"So, what are we watching?" Ray asked. "A show about a psychic." Gloria responded. "A psychic?" Ray questioned as he grabbed the bowl of chips from the coffee table. "Yeah, people are going to her to talk to loved ones who have moved on." Gloria answered as she grabbed some chips. "Well that sounds weird." Ray said with skepticism in his voice. "What? I think it is a great idea. Imagine if it worked." Gloria attacked Ray. "I think I want to try it. I think maybe we could talk to Alfred. Maybe she could bring him back." Gloria spoke with hope. "Bring him back? Gloria he is dead. We just have to keep living." Ray responded firmly. "Are you saying that she couldn't? If it were your brother you would explore all of the options." Gloria yelled. "Baby I'm saying even if somebody could they shouldn't. People should not mess with that stuff." Ray said calmly. "Well I'm going to do it. I'm going to find someone that can bring Alfred back. And if you don't want to fine, but I am." Gloria spoke in an elevated tone. "Well I love you but I don't think you should be messing around like this. Gloria you can't do this. You are creating false hope. Worse than that, you are considering meddling with something you shouldn't. what good could possibly come from resurrecting your brother even if you could?" Ray was getting agitated as well. "I thought you said you would do anything? What about it? Why won't you go with me? If it is fake and can't happen, why not?" Gloria screamed at him. "Look! Don't screw around with this stuff. I'm not going to do it. I hope it doesn't work but if it does, I don't want to be anywhere near it." Ray did his best to defend himself. "Chicken shit! Fine just go. I don't want you here. You don't love me! Just get out of my apartment!" Gloria was crying as she yelled. "Gloria." Ray tried to defuse her. "No leave!" Gloria was furious and pointed to the door. "I love you." Ray spoke as he got up. "Please don't do it Gloria. No good can come from this." Ray pleaded as he left. The door closed behind him and Gloria began to cry.

The next day Gloria started to do her research of where she would go to talk with a psychic. She looked on the internet and read reviews. Gloria also drove around and looked for shops to see how reliable they looked. It was a long day and she found no promising leads. Defeated, Gloria just decided to go to the grocery store to grab dinner.

She was about to call Ray and tell him how stupid it all was but then she noticed a lady staring at her. The women was an older lady with grey hair. She was wearing a long black dress with a shawl around her shoulders and a scarf on her head. The woman began to approach Gloria in a rapid pace. "Gloria my child I have been searching for you all day as you have been looking for me." The woman spoke. "How do you know my name?" Gloria questioned the stranger. "I had a vision that I was needed by a sad and confused girl named Gloria." The woman responded. "I knew I had to find you and help you for what you

are looking for is very dangerous. It is me
you need for this task." She continued.

"Okay you are freaking me out."
Gloria responded as she started to back up.
"Others play with the dead as if it is a game.
You need to be made aware of the risk." The
woman inched closer to Gloria. "Child you
should not be playing around with things
you do not know. Come and find me
tomorrow. We will talk more." The woman
continued. "But wait, how will I find you? I
don't even know your name." Gloria looked
intrigued and worried. "My name is Lucinda
Grady and here is my address. I will see you
tomorrow at noon. And Gloria please be
careful. Don't do anything until we meet
again." Lucinda answered as she handed
Gloria a business card with her information.

"See you tomorrow." Gloria said back as Lucinda disappeared into the crowd.

"Ray don't hang up." Gloria said on the phone. "I won't, just please don't try again. I'm serious, I won't be involved." Ray spoke sternly. "I have to. There was this lady at the store and she said that she had a vision that she needed to help me." Gloria almost pleaded with Ray to listen. "She even knew my name and told me to be careful." Gloria continued. "Look I love you. Please don't make me be a jerk." Ray ignored her attempt. "Are you going to come with me or not?" Gloria asked sharply. "No I am not and honestly you shouldn't either." Ray answered back matching her tone. "Fine then I will go without you." Gloria jabbed back with attitude. "If it goes bad just know

I'm staying away. You are messing with stuff you shouldn't." Ray lectured back.

"Are you breaking up with me?" Gloria asked with tears in her eyes. "I think you are breaking up with me." Ray responded.

"Gloria just don't do this." Ray continued.

"Well I have to." Gloria made her decision.

"Good bye Ray." Gloria finished and hung up the phone crying.

Chapter 2

The next day at noon Gloria decided to go see Lucinda Grady. She found the house quite easily. It was a small but cheerful house. There was a garden and it even it even had a porch. It was on that porch that Gloria saw Lucinda sitting and waving. "Hello!" Gloria beamed up at Lucinda. "Hello!" Lucinda cheerfully answered back. "The boyfriend said no?" Lucinda asked. "Yeah, he said I shouldn't be messing around with this stuff." Gloria answered with disappointment. "I really thought he would be here. I thought we were inseparable." Gloria continued as she sat down next to Lucinda. "Give him time. I'm sure he will come around. Now are you ready?" Lucinda comforted Gloria and motioned to the house. "As ready as I'll ever be." Gloria responded as she got up and followed Lucinda into the house.

The house was the exact opposite inside that it was on the outside. It was dark and there were items of the occult everywhere. In the center of the room was a table and Lucinda sat in a chair and directed Gloria to do the same. "Now I must warn you that Ray was right. You should not be playing with these things. But I know you are going to so I am willing to help. It is better that I do it than someone less experienced in these matters." Lucinda held Gloria's hand as she explained. "Now I can summon a soul from the other side but I must warn you that I cannot control which of the dead answer the calls of the living. I need you to concentrate for whomever you have the strongest attachment to from the event will be who comes back. You have to be sure that you think only of your brother." She continued. "Now go ahead and concentrate. Think about that night. Think about your brother. Focus. Focus all of your energy." Lucinda instructed. "Okay, I am thinking about that night." Gloria responded.

"Don't speak. Only think. Picture in your head." Lucinda warned. "Oh I feel it!" Lucinda blurted out. Then there was a crash from the other room. "He is here!" Lucinda yelled.

From the door to the kitchen walked out Kirk Smith. He was wielding a knife and he had locked eyes on Gloria. "How is it possible?" Gloria cried out. "Get out spirit! Get out of my house!" Lucinda yelled at Kirk. He walked towards Lucinda who began to speak but Kirk grabbed her and stabbed her in the abdomen. Kirk pulled out the knife and flipped over the table pinning Gloria to the ground with it. Lucinda who had fallen to the floor, grabbed a hold of Kirk's ankle. Lucinda was weak but still mustered up the strength to yell up at Kirk.

"I command you to leave. You are banished from this house!" She yelled. Kirk twitched a little bit and then something pulled him out of the room and back into the kitchen. Then they heard the sound of glass breaking as he was hurled out of Lucinda's house.

Gloria moved the table and got next to Lucinda. "Is he gone?" Gloria cried. "No. He is on his way to Ray now." Lucinda coughed as she tried to collect herself. "He was summoned and is now back part of this world." She continued. "He will not rest until he has had his fill of revenge." Lucinda told Gloria as she wiped away blood from her mouth. "Well what can I do?" Gloria asked in panic. "The only way to get rid of the spirit is for you and Ray to recreate the conditions of how he died. Only then will he return to the other side." Lucinda answered.

"Recreate the conditions of his death?"

Gloria repeated where she was confused.

"Yes, not necessarily the same place but

certainly he must be killed in exactly the

same way." Lucinda said as she continued to

bleed. "I'm afraid I'm not going to make it.

You must find Ray and end this." Lucinda

told Gloria who was now noticing the blood

pooling around Lucinda. "Go my child. Go

and find Ray. I am so sorry dear that this

happened." Lucinda spoke calmly as she

grabbed Gloria's hand. "I am sorry that I did

this. I can't believe I got you killed." Gloria

cried. "Be at peace. It was my time to go.

Do take care Gloria." Lucinda said this and

took a deep breath. She ceased moving and

Gloria knew she was dead.

Gloria sat there in panic for a moment and she wasn't sure what to do. She cried and she felt like she did that night when they went camping. Then she thought about the cop who was so nice to her and Ray. Gloria frantically called Officer Jennings who came over to the house rapidly. Gloria explained what happened and Jennings believed her. "Look I know it sounds crazy." Gloria explained. "I've been at this job a long time. It is not the weirdest thing I have ever heard." Jennings did his best to calm down Gloria. "I have to go find Ray." Gloria said. "We'll go together. If it is Kirk Smith it will be dangerous." Officer Jennings spoke confidently. "Come on, we'll take my car." He continued as he gave Gloria his jacket.

Chapter 3

Ray was fast asleep when he started to hear the voice. "Ray. Ray listen to me." The voice whispered. "Gloria needs your help." It continued. "No way, she did it to herself." Ray responded. "I am Lucinda Grady and we unleashed an unholy evil and Gloria needs your help to defeat it." Lucinda spoke. "Kirk Smith is coming for you. Help Gloria stop him or you will both be dead." She continued. "What? I didn't even do anything!" Ray yelled. "The dead do not care how they are back or who brought them back. They just want revenge on who sent them to the other side." Lucinda explained. "If not for Gloria at least save yourself. Kirk Smith is coming." Lucinda finished as Ray heard something at his door. Ray sprang up from bed and grabbed the bat next to his bedside table. He exited his room and approached the front door.

He looked through the peephole and saw Officer Jennings with Gloria standing behind him. Ray opened the door and the two of them entered the apartment. "Hey Ray." Officer Jennings said as he shook Ray's hand. "Ray." Gloria said as she ran up and hugged Ray. "I just had the weirdest dream." Ray spoke as he hugged her back. "Are you okay? I heard this voice of a lady called Lucinda Grady and she said Kirk Smith was back and you were in danger." Ray continued. "Yes, we did bring him back and Lucinda is dead." Gloria responded with a tear in her eye. "So what do we do?" Ray asked. "We have to recreate the conditions of his death." Gloria answered. "How are we going to do that?" Officer Jennings asked. "Well we are going to have to get him to the roof." Ray responded. "Are you in?" Gloria asked. "I really have no choice." Ray responded. "How do we get him here?" Jennings questioned. "He is coming for me apparently." Ray answered. "So do we just wait?" Gloria added in. When she said that there was a sound at the door.

"What was that?" Jennings asked. "It could be Kirk." Ray answered. "I'm going to go check." Jennings said as he pulled out his gun and approached the door. Jennings cracked the door and then it was kicked open the rest of the way and Kirk charged into the room. Jennings hit the ground and his gun flew out of his hand. It landed close to Gloria and she bent down to get it. Kirk lunged at her and grabbed her by her hair. "Leave her alone!" Ray yelled as he lifted up the bat to hit Kirk. The bat struck Kirk in the head and his hand released Gloria's hair. She grabbed the gun and crawled over to Officer Jennings.

Ray swung the bat again but Kirk caught it with his free hand and slashed at Ray with the knife in the other. Ray threw a punch at Kirk but it was blocked by the bat. Kirk then used the bat to take out Ray's legs. Kirk loomed over Ray and he threw the bat across the room. Kirk then lifted the knife over his head. "Freeze!" Officer Jennings yelled from the doorway behind Kirk. "I will shoot!" Jennings barked orders as Kirk turned towards him. Kirk started to move to

Jennings and Jennings opened fire. The bullet struck Kirk in the shoulder. "Ray get over here." Jennings told Ray. Ray got up and Jennings fired at Kirk again and this time he dropped him. Ray ran past Kirk's body and got to the hallway behind Jennings where Gloria was waiting. "You okay?" Ray asked her. "No." Gloria responded. "I'm so sorry." Gloria cried. "It's okay. I love you. We are going to be fine." Ray hugged Gloria as he tried to comfort her. "Okay kids we better get going." Jennings told the pair as Kirk was getting to his feet. "Let's move!" Jennings yelled and then fired at Kirk.

The shot missed and Kirk ran at Jennings and pulled him into the apartment. The door slammed behind them. Then the sounds of struggle. Jennings fired two shots but it was all for not. "Oh my God!" Jennings muffled screams could be heard through the door. "Run!" Jennings yelled. Then it was quiet. Blood began to flow from under the door and then it opened. Kirk walked out with Officer Jennings still on his knife. He flung Jennings to the ground and walked towards them. "Let's go!" Gloria yelled. Ray and Gloria made it to the stairs and Gloria pulled Ray to the roof. "What are you doing?" Ray asked. "We have to finish this! We have to get to the roof!" Gloria yelled back. They climbed the stairs as fast as they could with Kirk quietly stalking them the entire way. They made it to the door at the top of the stairs that said roof access. The pair went through it and slammed the door behind them.

"Ray I'm so sorry that I did this. I should never have done it. I got Lucinda killed and I got Officer Jennings killed. Now we might die." Gloria cried. "Hey it's okay. Let's just focus on living. What do we do?" Ray spoke calmly. "Well Lucinda said recreate his death so I guess we throw him off of the roof?" Gloria explained. "How are we going to get him off of the roof?" Ray asked. "Let's find a weapon." Gloria told Ray. They both looked around the roof for anything that could be used. "Here is a brick." Gloria said as she picked it up and handed it to Ray. "I'm going to lure him to the edge and you come up from behind and smack him with the brick." Gloria instructed. "It's worth a shot." Ray agreed.

117

The pair got into their positions as Kirk came through the door. "Hey Kirk!" Gloria yelled from the edge of the building. Kirk looked at her and darted towards her. Gloria got down on the ground. "Now!" She yelled. Ray came from around the chimney he was hiding behind and charged Kirk. Kirk turned and before Ray could swing the brick Kirk plunged the knife into Ray. Ray spit up blood and dropped to his knees. "Ray!" Gloria yelled and it drew Kirk's attention. Kirk turned to her and she began crying. Kirk was standing over her and was ready to kill. "I love you." Ray said to Gloria as he stood up. He lunged at Kirk and both of them toppled off of the roof.

Kirk landed on a parked car and Ray hit the sidewalk with a thud. "Ray!" Gloria yelled out. Gloria crawled over and looked down over the edge. Ray was not moving. He was dead. Gloria looked over and saw that Kirk had not moved as well. Broken glass had punctured his chest cavity and there was blood everywhere. Gloria ran downstairs to Ray's body. His face was smashed and he was a broken heap. Gloria broke down crying. The horrible ordeal was over. It wasn't until the next day that the cops arrived. A jogger had found Gloria holding Ray's dead body and crying hysterically. The cops had to pull her off of him. What started as a journey to bring back her brother became the nightmare that cost her the love of her life but she had survived Kirk Smith once more.

Made in the USA
Middletown, DE
05 June 2021

41145911R00071